THE PUPPY PLACE

DAISY

THE PUPPY PLACE

Don't miss any of these other stories by Ellen Miles!

Bandit
Baxter
Bear
Bella
Boomer
Buddy
Chewy and Chica
Cocoa
Cody
Cooper
Daisy
Flash
Gizmo
Goldie
Honey
Jack
Liberty
Lucky
Lucy
Maggie and Max
Mocha
Molly
Moose
Muttley
Noodle
Oscar
Patches
Princess
Pugsley
Rascal
Rocky
Scout
Shadow
Snowball
Stella
Sweetie
Teddy
Ziggy
Zipper

THE PUPPY PLACE

DAISY

ELLEN MILES

SCHOLASTIC INC.

For every kid who has been bullied and for those who speak up against it.

ISBN 978-0-545-72645-0

Cover art by Tim O'Brien
Original cover design by Steve Scott

12 11 10 9 8 7 6 5 15 16 17 18 19 20/0

Printed in the U.S.A. 40

First printing, November 2015

CHAPTER ONE

"Pink cupcakes," said Jasper, shaking his head. "Who brings pink cupcakes to school? I mean, what *boy* would bring them?"

"Pukey Diaper, that's who." Nicky shoved his coat into his cubby.

Jasper laughed. "Good old Pukey," he said. He shifted into a goo-goo baby voice. "Wah, wah, Mommy! Please bring pink cupcakes. It's Valentine's Day, Mommy!"

Charles, down by his own cubby, thought Jasper's imitation of a baby was pretty bad. Maybe he didn't have any younger brothers or sisters. Charles knew that his own brother, the

Bean, had never actually said "wah, wah, wah" in his life. And he had definitely never heard it from Luke Piper, the boy they were talking about. Charles looked around, hoping Luke was not nearby to hear the other boys making fun of him.

Luke was short and skinny, but he wasn't a baby. True, he had thrown up in class once — right after lunch, so it was kind of obvious that the spaghetti and meatballs had not agreed with him. That wasn't his fault. Anybody could get sick. But it had earned Luke a new nickname that seemed to be sticking: Pukey Luke.

Then somebody, Jasper maybe, had pointed out how Luke's mom always came along on field trips, and spent every Wednesday afternoon helping out during math class, and was always waiting to pick him up after school even though he lived close enough to walk home. "What, is he a baby who needs his mommy around all the time? Does

Piper need a new diaper?" Jasper had said one day out on the kickball field. And the rest of the nickname was born.

Their teacher, Mr. Mason, didn't know about it. In fact, not every kid in class knew. Jasper and Nicky were the main ones who used the mean name, and only quietly, when they were far from any grown-up or tattletale kid.

Charles had heard it, and he didn't like it. Luke was okay. He had an awesome Lego collection and could build just about anything. Once, for Sharing Circle he had brought in a whole Star Wars scene, with all the characters and everything.

If Luke had heard them call him Pukey Diaper, he didn't show it. He mostly ignored Nicky and Jasper, keeping his head down and his eyes on his schoolwork when they were whispering his name. Now he poked his head into the cubby area. "Cupcakes are ready," he told Charles.

"Better grab one. My mom's a really good baker. Plus, they're chocolate."

Charles noticed that Nicky and Jasper followed him right into the classroom, straight to the table where the cupcakes were set out on a pink-and-red tray. They pushed past Charles. Nicky took one and Jasper grabbed two.

"Uh-uh, Jasper," said Mr. Mason. "I think there are just enough for one each. Is that right, Mrs. Piper?"

Luke's mom nodded. "That's it for today," she said. "But if you tell me your birthday, I'll bake another batch then. Any flavor you want."

Jasper was too cool to be tempted by that. "Nah, that's okay," he said, backing away from the table. He licked the cupcake's frosting, and Charles saw a smear of pink on his nose. So much for thinking pink cupcakes were only for girls.

Anyway, not all girls were in love with pink. Charles's older sister, Lizzie, for example. She was not a "pink" kind of girl, not into fashion or princesses or unicorns. Lizzie was into dogs. She was the one who had convinced their parents that the Petersons should be a foster family for puppies. By now they had fostered many pups, taking care of each one for a little while, just until they could find it the perfect forever family.

Charles had to hand it to her: Lizzie could be convincing. She had even helped talk his parents into agreeing to adopt Buddy, the cutest and sweetest foster puppy ever. He was part of the family now and Charles's best friend.

"Cupcake, Charles?" Luke's mom smiled at him.

"Oh, thanks." Charles forgot about Buddy as he picked a cupcake from the tray. He peeled down the red paper and took a big bite. "Yum," he said.

The pink frosting was peppermint-flavored, and it went perfectly with the moist, rich chocolate cake. Charles's mom made cookies once in a while and a cake from a mix for every birthday, but she'd never made anything like this. Mrs. Piper really was a terrific baker.

Mrs. Piper beamed. "Glad you like it," she said. She reached out for Luke, standing near her, and pulled him into a hug. "Those are Lukey's favorites."

Charles felt his stomach tighten. He looked around, hoping that Jasper and Nicky were nowhere nearby. Fortunately, they were by the guinea pig cage, poking their chocolate-stained fingers at Huey, the class pet.

"Mom!" Luke made a face and pulled away from her. Charles saw his eyes flick toward Jasper and Nicky and knew Luke was thinking the same thing Charles was. It would be a disaster if those boys had seen and heard all that.

"Well, I guess that's my cue," said Mrs. Piper, laughing a little. She picked up the empty tray and headed out — luckily without any more public hugs.

After she left, Mr. Mason said it was time to pass out their valentines. Charles remembered Mom telling him how, when she was in second grade, she got only two cards on Valentine's Day — and Julie Schweizer, the most popular girl in class, got thirty-four. That would never happen in room 2B, since everybody was supposed to give cards to everyone else. By the time they'd all run around the room passing out their cards, every desk had the same good-sized stack.

Charles opened his cards quickly. Most of them were pretty silly, but he liked the ones featuring dogs or cats. The one from Jasper had a robot army guy on it.

He looked at Luke, who sat kitty-corner from him at their group of desks. Luke hadn't opened a single card. He just sat there, staring down at the top envelope on his pile. Charles could read the black scrawly lettering from where he sat. *Pukey Diaper*, it said.

That afternoon, when Charles walked out of school, he spotted Mom's van parked in the pickup zone. What was she doing there? Charles usually walked home. He ran over and hopped in.

"Good day, honey?" Mom asked.

Charles thought for a second. That wasn't an easy question to answer. He had liked the cupcakes and the valentines. He didn't like remembering the look on Luke's face as he'd stared down at that card. He shrugged.

“Okay, then,” said Mom. Sometimes she understood when Charles didn’t feel like talking. She started the van and drove up the street. “Aren’t you going to ask me where we’re going?”

“Dentist?” Charles asked. “Eye doctor?” He didn’t remember having an appointment, but that was nothing new.

“Try ‘puppy,’” Mom said.

Charles stared at her. “Puppy?” he asked.

She nodded. “Looks like we have a new dog to foster.” She grinned at him. “So, *now* is it a good day?”

CHAPTER TWO

Charles laughed. "Sure, it's great!" he said. "But where's the puppy coming from?"

Mom sighed. "It's kind of a long story, but remember my friend Wilma who works at the paper?"

"The lady at the front desk?" Charles loved to visit the *Littleton News* offices with his mom. It was pretty cool that she was a reporter for the local newspaper, even if she did mostly write about boring stuff like school board meetings and town budget issues. He always liked seeing her name underneath a headline: *By Betsy Peterson.*

"Right, she's the receptionist. She's worked there for longer than anyone else, even the editor." Mom shook her head. "Wilma could probably put out that newspaper all by herself if she had to. Anyway, she's been telling me for a while about this new puppy her daughter was going to get."

"What kind?" Charles asked.

Mom thought for a second. "Some kind of terrier? I can't remember for sure. It's a little dog, I know that. And very cute, apparently."

Mom was really more of a cat person, so it wasn't surprising she hadn't paid attention to the puppy's breed. Charles smiled. He liked little dogs. Lizzie was into the big breeds, but Charles loved dogs who could fit on your lap or be carried around. "So did they get it?" he asked.

Mom nodded. "They've had it for a few months, and I guess things aren't really working out so well. That's why they want us to foster."

"Wait," said Charles. "I hate calling a puppy 'it.' Is it a girl or a boy?"

Mom thought again. "A girl. Right, a girl. Because I know her name is Daisy."

"Okay," said Charles. It was always exciting to hear about a new puppy coming to stay. "So what's the problem?"

Mom frowned. "Well, I'm not really sure. It sounded like everything was going well for a while. Wilma's daughter was crazy about the puppy. Her kids loved the puppy, and so did her husband. But then . . . as I said, I'm not really sure. Wilma just said something about them feeling overwhelmed."

Charles nodded. He knew how much work puppies could be.

"So Wilma begged me to take Daisy and try to find her a good home. It's not a great time for us, between your dad having Rookie Week at the firehouse and my project, but how could I say no? Wilma has done lots of favors for me. As long as the puppy is as little trouble as she says, things should be fine."

Charles knew that his mom was very busy writing a special Spring Events article for the *Littleton News*, and that his dad would be working extra-long hours, since there were new firefighters to be trained. The Bean would be spending a lot of extra time at Penny's Place, his day-care center, and Lizzie would be busy in the afternoons with her dog-walking business. "I'll spend every minute with the puppy when I'm home," Charles promised. "Anyway, we have to take her. You don't want her to have to go to the shelter, do you? We're a foster family. It's what we do."

"It's what we do," Mom agreed. She pulled up in front of a small brick house. "Before we go in, is there anything you want to tell me? You looked a little upset when you got into the car."

Charles shook his head. He didn't want to think about it right then. Anyway, it was no big deal. He'd heard all about bullying and how you weren't supposed to do it, and how you should tell an adult if you heard about it — but it wasn't really bullying just to tease somebody a little, was it? Luke was fine. Everything was fine. "I'm fine," he told Mom. "Let's go meet Daisy." He unbuckled his seat belt and climbed out of the car.

A frazzled-looking lady opened the door just seconds after Mom knocked. "Oh, wonderful," she said, pushing a cloud of frizzy hair out of her face. She held a toddler on her hip, and another, younger baby crawled around at her feet. Both kids' faces were smeared with purple: Grape jelly? Finger paint? *Who could tell?* thought Charles. Both wore stained T-shirts over saggy diapers, and their hair stood up in tangled spikes. "You must be Mrs. Peterson."

Mom nodded. "Betsy. And this is my son Charles."

Charles stuck out his hand, the way he'd been taught. "Nice to meet —" he began, but just then a squirmy, wriggly, and totally adorable black-and-white puppy ran between the woman's legs. The pup looked like she was about to make a break for it, right out the front door. Charles acted fast. He swooped down and blocked her way, opening his arms wide. "Here, Daisy," he called. She leapt right into his arms and immediately began to lick his face all over. Her darting tongue went into his nose, his eyes, and even his ears.

Hi! Hi! Hi! I love attention. Any kind of attention. Especially from someone like you. I can tell you love dogs. You're really going to love me.

Charles plopped down on the floor, giggling. He held Daisy's muscly body tight, even though she tried to squirm and worm her way out of his grasp. She was so cute, with her smushed-in little face, her bulging black eyes, and her pointy, perky ears. Her short coat was soft, and her stubby tail did not stop wagging. Charles petted Daisy while he waited for the woman to invite them in.

That didn't happen. Instead of opening the door wider, the woman handed Mom a thin pink leash. "Great. This is great. I'm so glad you can help us out. She's a cutie, but it's just too much. Who knew that a puppy could create so much trouble?"

Mom cleared her throat. "Well," she began.

The crawling baby tried to stand up, fell down on his butt, and dropped his bottle. He started to wail. The toddler joined in, screeching at the top of his lungs. Their mom rolled her eyes. "I don't know what we were thinking, getting a puppy. I honestly don't. I've got my hands more than full just with these guys. There's just no way I can care for a dog, too."

"Is there anything we should know about Daisy?" Mom had to shout to be heard over the din the two kids made.

The woman shrugged. "Not really," she said. "She eats regular kibble, and she's all toilet trained and everything. She's very sweet and sensitive. She loves to cuddle the boys when they're crying, and she always cheers them up." She jiggled the toddler in her arms. "Shhh, shhh," she said. "They'll miss her, but hopefully they're too young to remember her for long. Anyway, she's great. She's just — you know — a puppy." She looked as if she was about to say something else, but instead she flashed a bright smile at Charles and his mom. "Well — thanks again." She started to close the door. "Bye!"

“Uh, okay,” said Mom.

Charles clipped Daisy’s leash to her collar. “I guess you’re coming with us,” he said. Daisy trotted along happily by his side. She leapt into the van the second he opened the door, and settled herself next to Charles.

“Interesting,” said Charles as he and Mom drove off. “They couldn’t wait to see her go, and she couldn’t wait to leave.” He couldn’t blame Daisy, if the house was always that noisy and busy.

Mom frowned at the dog on Charles’s lap. “Why do I have the feeling that there’s something she wasn’t telling us?” she asked.

CHAPTER THREE

"Ooh! Ooh! That is the most adorable dog in the entire universe."

"Let me hold her!"

"No, me!"

"Look at her darling eyes."

Daisy curled tighter into Charles's arms. He had carried her into the house so she would feel secure and not overwhelmed by a new place, and now there were four girls shrieking and waving their hands at her. Lizzie and her friends Maria, Daphne, and Brianna had been sitting at the kitchen table, but they all jumped up when they saw Daisy.

“A new puppy?” Lizzie asked. “Are we fostering her? Why didn’t I get to come when you picked her up? What’s her name?”

Charles wasn’t sure which question to answer first. “Daisy,” he said. “And quiet down. You’re scaring her.”

Lizzie got hold of herself. “Oops,” she said. “I was just . . . excited.”

“No, really?” Mom asked with a smile. “Anyway, yes. She is a foster puppy. You didn’t get to come because you had something else planned.” She nodded at the other girls. “Your business meeting?”

Originally, the dog-walking business had just been Lizzie and Maria’s. The two of them had never needed to have meetings, since they were best friends and together all the time anyway. But since Brianna and Daphne had joined them, things had gotten a little more official. Lizzie had even had business cards printed, with LIZZIE PETERSON, PRESIDENT written on them.

Now nobody was thinking about business. They were all focused on Daisy. "She's a Boston terrier," said Lizzie, reaching out to gently scratch Daisy between the ears. "The first one I ever met." She closed her eyes, and Charles knew that she was picturing her "Dog Breeds of the World" poster, trying to remember what it said about the breed. "The American Gentleman, they're called," she reported after a moment. "Even when they're girls, I guess! Because they're one of the first dogs ever bred in America. Plus, they're so stylish, with their short black-and-white coats. And look at those perky ears. She really is a cutie."

Daisy blinked her big black bulgy eyes and licked Lizzie's hand with a tiny pink tongue, and all the girls sighed. "Awww," they said. "Ohhhh."

Charles smiled. How hard could it be to find a forever home for this cutie? Everybody loved her the minute they met her. He wondered how she and Buddy would get along. "Buddy," he called. "Come meet a new friend." Buddy was always nice to the Petersons' foster puppies, even when some of them — like Oscar, a grouchy Schnauzer they'd fostered recently — weren't so nice to him.

Buddy bounded into the kitchen and screeched to a halt when he saw the pup in Charles's arms. He stretched his neck up to sniff her, and Daisy stretched her neck down to sniff him. Their noses met and Buddy's tail started to wag.

"He likes her," said Charles. He knelt to let Daisy down, and she immediately went into a play bow, front paws stretched out and tiny puppy butt in the air. Then she jumped on top of Buddy.

Buddy stepped back and stared at her, and she bowed and jumped again. Charles wondered how

Buddy would feel about this little one who seemed to think she was a big, tough dog. Would he decide to put her in her place?

Buddy looked up at Charles. He looked back at Daisy. He gave one little woof. And then he rolled onto the floor on his back, four legs waving in the air.

Everybody burst out laughing. "I guess he's just going to let her boss him around," Lizzie said. "How cute is that?"

"The lady who gave her up said she's really sweet and sensitive," Charles said. He didn't want anyone thinking that Daisy was a bully.

Lizzie nodded. "Bostons are supposed to be terrific companions," she said. "They just want to be with their people." She looked at her watch and gasped. "You guys," she said. "We'd better get going. We have a lot of dogs waiting for their walks."

The girls said good-bye to Daisy and took off, leaving the house peaceful and quiet. "I'll be up in my office," said Mom. "You'll watch Daisy, right?"

"Of course," said Charles. But he could already see that Daisy wouldn't need much watching. She was a good girl; he could tell. "Aren't you?" he asked her, scooping her up into his arms.

She wriggled with delight and nibbled on his chin.

I am! I am a good girl. Mostly.

Charles took both puppies out back and made sure Daisy knew where to do her business. Then he settled into the living room to play with them, lying on the rug as the puppies wrestled and dashed around the couch. Buddy pulled each of his toys out of the toy basket in turn, showing them off to Daisy. She especially seemed to like

Mr. Duck, Buddy's favorite toy. When she grabbed it and ran around the room with it, Buddy looked at Charles with big eyes, obviously hoping for help with the problem.

Charles felt sorry for him. He knew how much Buddy loved Mr. Duck. "It's okay, Buddy," Charles said. "Be a nice boy and share your toys." Buddy seemed to give a doggy shrug. He went to his basket and pulled out a ball, and the two pups lay near each other on the rug, playing happily.

"You two will be fine together for a few minutes," said Charles. "Right?" They both looked up at him with innocent eyes. Charles laughed and went into the kitchen to grab a snack.

When he came back into the living room with an apple in his hand, Charles gasped.

Mr. Duck was history.

CHAPTER FOUR

Charles stared in horror at the shredded bits and pieces on the floor, arranged in a scattered circle as if a little bomb had exploded. Buddy gazed up at Charles, brow furrowed and a quizzical tilt to his head, as if he were wondering what had happened.

Next to him sat Daisy, looking up at Charles with big round black eyes. Her stubby tail twitched just a little as she posed innocently next to the wreckage of Buddy's all-time favorite toy. She cocked her head and gave him a doggy smile.

I didn't do anything. At least, I didn't mean *to do anything. You're not upset with me, are you?*

Charles just ignored Daisy. He was upset, but it was too late to punish her: the damage was done. Instead, he bent to hug Buddy. "I'm sorry, pal. We'll get you a new Mr. Duck, I promise." He still couldn't believe that Mr. Duck had finally bitten the dust. The toy had been through a lot: his stuffing was missing, his wings were floppy, and his beak was grayish and scarred by chewing. But now? Charles couldn't even tell which piece of fluff might have been part of a wing, or tail, or beak.

He heard Mom's footsteps on the stairs and quickly bent to scoop the shreds into a small pile that he sat on, pulling Daisy into his lap. Mom didn't need to know about this, not right then.

She'd already made it clear that she was not up for a foster puppy with "issues."

"How's it going?" Mom asked as she walked through the living room on her way to the kitchen.

"Great," said Charles. "Just great."

By the time Charles left for school on Monday morning, he and Lizzie had discovered and cleaned up three or four small "Daisy bombs," as they had come to call them. A paper towel, a dish-rag, one of the Bean's mittens, and something that might have once been a pot holder had all been carefully torn to shreds.

Mom was right. Daisy's owners had not told them everything about her. And now, by cleaning up the messes without telling Mom, Charles felt like he was only passing along the lie.

"It's not exactly a lie," Lizzie had said. "It's just . . . not the whole truth. If Mom knew, she might make us give Daisy up, and we'd have to take her to Caring Paws. Daisy would hate it at the shelter."

Charles knew his sister was right. The animal shelter where Lizzie regularly volunteered was comfortable and clean. But the animals there spent a lot of time alone in their kennels. "I know," Charles agreed. "She'd be miserable if she couldn't be near people all the time." Still, he did not feel comfortable keeping Daisy's destructive habit a secret.

It was kind of like the thing with Luke Piper and the way certain kids teased him. Charles had thought a lot about it over the weekend, and he knew it was wrong to keep quiet about that, too. At recess the next day, Charles sat near the jungle gym with his friends David and Sammy. They were both in Mr. Mason's room, and they had also heard Luke being teased.

"It's not fair," David said. "Luke's a good guy.

Why do they have to pick on him?" He looked at Luke, who was sitting on the wide wooden stairs near the school's back door, reading a book. Luke didn't usually join in the daily kickball games or play four square or climb on the jungle gym. He seemed happier hanging out on his own.

"Should we tell Mr. Mason?" Sammy asked. "I hate to be a tattletale, but those guys make me mad."

Charles thought. "Or maybe I could tell Nicky and Jasper to leave him alone." The thought made his stomach hurt, since he had a feeling about how that would go. Probably Nicky and Jasper would just start picking on him instead.

"Let's watch and wait," said David. "If they bug Luke again, we'll make sure Mr. Mason knows about it."

Charles and Sammy nodded. "That sounds

good," said Sammy. "It's a deal." He stuck out his hand, and they did a three-way shake.

The bell rang, and everybody ran to line up. Mr. Mason opened the doors and they streamed inside, talking and laughing until he reminded them to stay in line and keep quiet and — "No running, Nicky."

They were just getting settled in their classroom when they heard the sirens. The screaming, wailing sound drew closer and closer; then brakes screeched and the sirens stopped. Car doors slammed and there was the sound of running footsteps. "Stay seated, kiddos!" called Mr. Mason, but it was too late. Everyone was already at the windows, staring out as the ambulance guys in their blue suits ran into the playground.

"What do you think happened?" Charles whispered to Sammy.

“I don’t know,” said Sammy. “But did you notice who’s missing?” He waved a hand at the line of kids along the windows, and Charles looked up and down the row.

Luke Piper was not in the classroom.

CHAPTER FIVE

Charles's stomach did a flip. "Where's Luke?" he whispered to Sammy.

Sammy shrugged.

Charles looked around the room for Nicky and Jasper. There they were, at the window with everyone else. He clenched his fists. Had they done something to Luke? If they had, it was partly Charles's fault, because he had not spoken up about it when they teased Luke. His stomach flipped again.

Mr. Mason clapped his hands. "Okay, let's step away from the windows. This isn't a movie. Nothing to see. Everyone back to their desks."

Slowly, everybody sat down in their places, but the room was filled with an excited buzz of voices. Everyone was talking at once.

Mr. Mason clapped his hands again. "Quiet down, kiddos. And pull out your math workbooks. I'm going down to the office to find out what's happening, but meanwhile I want you to get busy." He told them to open to page thirty-two and begin on the problems there.

Charles nudged Sammy, who sat next to him. "What do you think happened?" he whispered.

Sammy shook his head. "Could be anything," he said. "Maybe aliens landed in the playground right after we went inside."

Mr. Mason cleared his throat. When Charles looked up, his teacher was staring right at him. Charles picked up his pencil and started to work on the first problem on the page.

Mr. Mason said a few quiet words to Mrs. Weiss, the classroom helper. Then he clapped his hands for attention again. "I'll be back in a few minutes. Listen to Mrs. Weiss and keep working on your problems, and I'll be back before you know it."

After Mr. Mason left, Charles sat staring at his workbook, chewing on his pencil and thinking. He had a bad feeling about this. Where was Luke? What had happened out on the playground? He hoped Mr. Mason would explain things when he got back.

Not many math problems got done while Mr. Mason was gone. There was a lot of whispering and getting up to sharpen pencils or say hi to Huey, and Nicky and Jasper started to sword fight with their rulers. "Quiet down, people," said Mrs. Weiss. "Let's settle down." But her voice barely rose over the noise in the classroom, and when she clapped her hands, nobody really paid attention.

Instead, the buzz in the room got louder and louder until Mr. Mason walked back in, shutting the door firmly behind him and standing with his hands on his hips. He shook his head, looking disappointed, as he waited for the classroom to quiet down.

"That's better," he said, when everyone was seated and quiet. "But next time, when I ask you to listen to Mrs. Weiss, I expect you to do just that." He walked to his desk and sat down on the edge. "I know you're all wondering what happened," he said. "It's nothing to worry about. Nobody was hurt. But there's something I need to explain to you."

Charles put his pencil down. That sounded serious. Even Nicky and Jasper sat up straight, listening closely.

"Mr. Stephano called the ambulance because he saw something happen in the playground, just after everyone lined up."

Mr. Stephano was one of the playground monitors. He mostly stood around talking into his walkie-talkie. Once Charles had heard him asking someone — one of the cafeteria ladies? — what was for lunch. And once he had broken up a fight that had started during a kickball game, when some kids were arguing over whether a ball had been foul or not.

"What happened was that Luke Piper had a seizure," Mr. Mason continued.

There were a few loud gasps in the room, but most kids just looked confused. Then Sammy asked the question on everyone's mind. "What's that?"

"I'll explain." Mr. Mason stood up and started to pace. "Luke has a condition called epilepsy, which can cause problems with the way his brain sometimes works."

Charles thought he remembered hearing that word "epilepsy" before, but he did not know what it meant. From the looks on their faces, none of his classmates did, either.

"Our brains have electrical signals going off all the time," said Mr. Mason. "Signals that tell our muscles and the rest of our body what to do." He went to the chalkboard and drew a head, with some lightning-bolt marks inside it. "But sometimes, in people who have epilepsy, there are too many signals all at once and everything gets overloaded. It's like a storm in the brain." He drew a whole bunch more lightning bolts. "When that happens, the person's muscles might do some strange things, like tighten and relax very quickly. The person might shake, or fall down. Or sometimes, with a small seizure, they might just stare into space for a few seconds."

Nicky threw his hand up. "Is it catching?" he asked.

Mr. Mason shook his head. "Absolutely not. Scientists are still not sure why epilepsy happens, but it is not contagious. And Luke may not have seizures all his life, either. Some people seem to grow out of epilepsy as they age."

Charles put his hand up. "Is Luke okay?" he asked.

Mr. Mason nodded. "He fell down, but he didn't hurt himself. And once a seizure is over, it's over. The person might feel a little strange for a while, but soon they feel all right again. He'll probably be back at school tomorrow. Luke takes medicine to control his seizures, but according to his mother, he was late to school today and forgot to take it."

Charles sat back in his seat. Suddenly, he understood why Luke's mom hung around the school so much, and why he didn't climb high up on the jungle gym. It must be scary to have epilepsy and never know when you might have a seizure.

"What do we do if we see someone having a seizure?" David asked.

"Excellent question," said Mr. Mason. "First of all, make sure you let an adult know what's happening. You can help the person lie down, and give him — or her — space. The seizure will pass on its own. There's a lot more to learn about this," Mr. Mason said, "but maybe we'll let Luke and his mom tell us another day. For now, let's get on with our work and just be happy that he's okay."

Charles went back to his math workbook, but it was not easy to concentrate. He thought about Luke, sitting by himself in the playground. He thought about how he had not spoken up when Nicky and Jasper teased Luke. He thought about how hard it must be to have epilepsy and feel different from everyone else. And he made himself a promise: next time he saw him, Charles was going to make sure that Luke Piper knew he had a friend.

CHAPTER SIX

He could tell. The moment he walked through the front door of his house that afternoon, Charles knew there was something wrong. For one thing, where was Buddy? The little brown pup was always waiting at the door when Charles got home from school. And if there was a foster puppy in the house, the two dogs would be waiting together. Not that day. This was not good.

No Buddy, no Daisy, and a house that was very, very quiet. *Too* quiet.

"Mom?" Charles called.

"Up here," she called back from upstairs.

Charles headed up to Mom's study. "Where's —" he began, but then he saw her. Daisy, behind the bars of a metal crate. Charles raised his eyebrows. Of course the Petersons had a crate. Lizzie said it was one of the best dog-training tools around. But with five people around to keep an eye on things, they rarely had to use it — except with puppies who weren't housebroken yet or who had terrible behavior problems.

Daisy gazed at Charles, her bulgy black eyes all innocent.

Don't be mad, please. I didn't mean to do it.

"What did she do?" Charles asked. "Can I let her out?" When Mom nodded, he opened the door of the crate. He sat down on the floor and Daisy jumped into his lap.

"She was fine until lunchtime," his mom said. "She and Buddy played together. She kept stealing his toys, but he was okay with it. Then they napped together. It was cute, really."

Charles knew there was a "but" coming. "But?" he asked.

"I went downstairs to make myself a sandwich for lunch. Buddy came with me, but she stayed up here." Mom frowned at Daisy. "And she took every single piece of paper out of my wastebasket and chewed it up. Totally shredded it. It looked like a bomb went off in here."

Charles felt relief wash over him. Another Daisy bomb, but she hadn't destroyed anything important. He petted Daisy's head, and she snorted happily, seeming to sense that she was forgiven. "So it was just trash, anyway," he said. "No big deal."

"No big deal this time," Mom said. "But I can't have a destructive dog roaming free in the house. What if she'd destroyed my notes for the story I'm working on, the way Jack did that time?"

Jack was a boxer the Petersons had fostered, who had tried to eat just about everything he saw. No wonder Daisy made Mom nervous.

"Or what if she ruined something even more valuable?" Mom peered at Charles. "You don't seem too surprised. Did you know something about this?"

Charles gulped and pulled Daisy closer. "Well," he said. "Sort of. Maybe."

Mom rolled her eyes. "Charles," she said. "We've talked about this before. Keeping things from me is pretty much the same as lying."

Charles looked down at his sneakers. "I'm sorry," he said.

"I knew there was something Wilma's daughter wasn't telling me." Mom sighed and sat back in her chair. "What are we going to do now? I don't want to have to keep her in the crate all day. She might as well be at Caring Paws if we're going to do that."

"I'll watch her every minute when I'm home," Charles promised, eager to make up for his mistake. "And — and I'll call Aunt Amanda and ask her what to do." Charles's aunt ran a doggy day care and knew all about every kind of puppy problem you could imagine.

Mom nodded. "All right," she said. "Buddy's out in the backyard, by the way. I'm sure they'd love some playtime together." She turned back to her computer, but Charles didn't move.

She spun around in her chair and looked at him. "Charles," she said. "Is there something else you haven't told me?"

It all spilled out. Charles petted Daisy's soft, short fur as he told Mom all about Luke, and the teasing, and the seizure.

"Oh, honey," Mom said. She held out her arms, and Charles went to sit in her lap, still holding Daisy. Mom hugged him close. "You should have told me right away when you heard those kids bullying Luke. But I'm glad you decided to stand up for what was right. And then he had a seizure. That must have been scary for everyone."

"It was," said Charles, rubbing his nose into the plush fur of Daisy's neck. She snuffled at him softly, as if she was comforting him.

It's okay. Don't worry.

Charles kissed Daisy. It was amazing how a dog could make you feel better. Daisy seemed to know exactly how he was feeling. He thought again about the sirens. "Probably it was scariest for Luke."

"Why don't you invite him over?" Mom asked. "I bet he'd like to meet Daisy."

At her name, Daisy began to squirm, wriggling her way out of his arms. "Good idea," said Charles. "I'll call him later. But right now I'd better get this girl outside." His mom gave him one last squeeze and let him off her lap.

"No more secrets, right?" she asked him.

He stuck out his hand for a shake. "No more secrets."

After he'd played with both puppies in the backyard for a while, Charles called his aunt. "What do you do if you have a puppy who wants to chew things up?" he asked.

"Uh-oh," said Aunt Amanda.

"She's not eating things, like Jack," Charles said. "She just, like, destroys stuff."

"Got it," said Aunt Amanda. "Well, for one thing, you need to keep an eye on her. Don't give her the chance to chew things up. If you see her chewing on something she shouldn't, you can swap it for something it's okay to chew on, like a Kong toy."

"But I can't be with her every second," said Charles.

"Funny you should say that," said Aunt Amanda. "Some people *do* stay with destructive dogs every second when they're training them. It's called tethering. They keep the dog leashed by their side all day."

"I don't think Mr. Mason would let me have Daisy with me at school," Charles said.

"Guess not." Aunt Amanda laughed. "So she'll also have to spend some time in a crate. Hopefully this is just a phase she is going through, and she'll grow out of it soon."

Charles watched Daisy closely for the rest of the day, even after Lizzie came home from walking dogs. He felt like the little pup was his responsibility. If she kept destroying things, how would they ever find her a forever home?

CHAPTER SEVEN

Luke was back in class the day after his seizure, seeming just the same as always. Charles had called to ask him over, and he had agreed eagerly, after checking with his mother. Now, after school, they got ready to head to Charles's.

"You're so lucky you get to walk home from school every day." Luke grabbed his backpack out of his cubby. "I wish my mom would let me do that."

Charles had never thought that walking home from school was anything special. But maybe it was if you weren't allowed to do it. "When the weather's nice, I ride my bike," he said. "Would she let you do that?"

Luke shook his head. "Probably not. She'd keep me in a bubble if she could."

Life in a bubble did not sound like much fun at all. Still, Charles could understand why Luke's mom might worry about him. What if he had a seizure when he was by himself? He could get hurt if he fell down. "I guess your mom just wants you to be safe," Charles said.

"Some kids with epilepsy have so many seizures that they have to wear a helmet all the time to protect their heads," Luke said. "At least she doesn't make me do that."

They headed to Charles's house, kicking a soccer ball back and forth between them as they walked. When the ball took a high bounce off the curb, Luke put out his hands to catch it. "Another thing I'm not allowed to do," Luke said. "I can't head the ball."

"I'm not supposed to, either," Charles said. Dad had told him that using his head to pass a soccer ball was not a good idea until he was grown up, and maybe not even then. "It's okay. It gives us more time to practice with our feet."

They walked in silence for a few blocks. Charles felt a little shy around Luke, and he could tell that Luke felt the same way.

"I brought some Legos," Luke said finally.

"Great," Charles said. "Maybe you can show me how you made that bulldozer." Luke had brought in three trucks he'd made, to show at Sharing Circle that day. "Even Jasper had to admit that was pretty cool." He watched Luke's face, to see how he reacted to Jasper's name.

Luke rolled his eyes. "Jasper," he said with a snort. "First he bullied me. Now he's scared of me."

"Scared?" Charles asked.

"Sure," said Luke. "They're all scared. Everybody's treating me like I'm made out of glass. They don't even want to come close to me in case I have a seizure." He kicked the ball extra hard and it flew into some prickly bushes.

"That stinks." Charles helped pull back branches so Luke could reach in and get the ball.

"Whatever," said Luke. Then he was quiet again for the rest of the walk.

The silence ended when they got home to find Buddy and Daisy waiting at the door. "Hey, there," Luke said, kneeling right down so both dogs could climb into his lap and lick his face. "Oh, man, they're both so cute." He held Buddy's paw. "This one is Buddy, right? And you" — he picked up Daisy and held her in his arms like a baby — "you must be the famous Daisy." She gazed up at him, snorting happily while her big ears twitched. She licked his chin until he giggled.

You look like you could use some big love — from a little dog!

Charles had been telling his classmates about Daisy at Sharing Circle each morning. "Right, that's her," he said. "Wow, you love dogs, don't you?"

"They're the best," said Luke. "We used to have one when I was really little. She was a black Lab named Nora. I used to take naps with her every day. Mom was really, really sad when she died."

"Maybe your parents are ready for a new dog," Charles said. Luke and Daisy made a terrific pair. What if the Pipers adopted Daisy?

"Actually —" Luke started to say something but stopped.

Charles saw Luke close his eyes and bite his lip. Was he — was he about to have a seizure? Charles was about to yell for his mom when

Luke's eyes opened. "Actually what?" Charles asked him.

Luke shook his head. "Nothing," he said. He put Daisy down and reached out for Buddy. "C'mere, you. You need some petting, too."

Mom came down the stairs. "Hi, Luke," she said. "It's nice to have you here."

"Hi, Mrs. Peterson," said Luke. "I guess Daisy was a good girl today, huh? Otherwise she would be in the crate again."

Charles's mom laughed. "Has Charles been giving reports at Sharing Circle? Well, yes. As a matter of fact, she's been very good, as long as I don't let her out of my sight. She only had to spend an hour or two in the crate today, while I was out doing an interview." Mom headed for the kitchen. "Come find me when you're ready for a snack," she called over her shoulder.

Charles sat down on the floor next to Luke and pulled Daisy into his lap. "What a good girl," he said. She wriggled all over with happiness. "All you want is to be around people, isn't that right?" he asked her. "You don't like to be alone."

"I don't, either," said Luke quietly. "I wonder if she's scared to be alone. I am, sometimes."

Charles could understand that. If he had epilepsy, he might be afraid sometimes, too. "Wouldn't it be great if you had a dog to be with you all the time?" he asked.

Luke nodded. "Sure," he said. Charles noticed that he squeezed his eyes shut again for a moment. He wondered if Luke was making a wish — a wish for a dog like Daisy.

After their snack, Charles and Luke spent the rest of afternoon playing with the puppies. Luke's Legos stayed in his backpack as the boys raced around the backyard and threw balls for Daisy and Buddy. Both puppies — and both boys — were tired out by the time Luke's mom came to pick him up.

That night, Mom came to tuck Charles in. "Seems like you and Luke had a pretty good time today," she said.

"Yeah." Charles rubbed his eyes. He was very sleepy. "And he loves Daisy." He drifted off to sleep, feeling sure that he had found the perfect home for the black-and-white pup.

CHAPTER EIGHT

Luke was not at school the next morning, and Charles wondered if he was okay. “Is Luke sick?” he asked Mr. Mason as they were taking their places for Sharing Circle. They always sat “criss-cross applesauce” in a circle on the solar system rug. Charles always liked to sit as close as he could to Mars, his favorite planet. That day he was right next to it, perched on Phobos. That was one of Mars’s moons.

“Luke is fine,” said Mr. Mason. “In fact, Luke has a very special surprise for us today. He’ll be coming in right after lunch.”

“What’s the surprise?” asked Bethany.

Charles groaned. Why did somebody always have to ask that? The whole point of a surprise was that it was a surprise.

Mr. Mason just raised his eyebrows and grinned. "If I told you," he began, and the class yelled out the rest: "It wouldn't be a surprise!"

Charles had a hard time paying attention to his work that morning. He kept wondering what Luke's surprise could be. The hours dragged on until — finally — lunchtime and recess were over. When they got back into the classroom, Luke was still not there. "Settle down, everyone," said Mr. Mason. "While we wait for Luke, let's go over our spelling words from yesterday."

Charles noticed that he was not the only one glancing at the door every few minutes. Even Mr. Mason seemed excited and distracted. He gave them the same spelling word twice in a row and didn't even notice until David pointed it out.

Then Charles heard a knock on their classroom door. Mr. Mason jumped up and ran to open it. The whole class jumped up, too, and clustered near the door. "Well, hello," said Mr. Mason. "Welcome to room 2B."

Luke walked into the classroom holding one end of a leash. At the other end was a beautiful dog — a tall, broad-chested German shepherd with a long, feathery tail and huge pointed ears. He looked like a superhero in his orange-and-blue vest.

"Wow," said Charles under his breath. That was some dog. He noticed that a few kids in the room seemed to pull back, as if they were afraid. Jasper was one of them. He crossed his arms and stared at the dog.

"This is Hugo," Luke said proudly. "He's my new seizure dog."

Charles let out a gasp. He couldn't help it. He had been so sure that Luke would adopt Daisy —

but instead he had this dog. Where had Hugo come from?

Luke met Charles's eyes and gave him a special smile. "I have been on a waiting list for three years," he said. "Ever since I found out I have epilepsy. We heard this week that my dog might be ready for me, but I didn't tell anyone. I was afraid to jinx it."

Charles grinned back. Now he understood why Luke had acted that way — closing his eyes and biting his lip — when they had talked about dogs. "He's great-looking. What does a seizure dog do?" Charles asked. He was itching to pet Hugo's noble-looking head.

"That's what Luke is here to explain to us," Mr. Mason said. "And his mom and Ms. Danvers, too."

Now Charles noticed the two women who had come in behind Luke and Hugo.

“Ms. Danvers was one of Hugo’s trainers,” explained Luke’s mom. “She works for a group called Happy Helpers that matches dogs with people who need them.”

Ms. Danvers gave everyone a little wave. “Hi there,” she said. “Just so you know, there is no need to be afraid of Hugo. He’s very, very well trained and very gentle.”

Charles glanced at Jasper. He did not look completely convinced by what Ms. Danvers had said, but he did uncross his arms and take a step or two closer to the dog.

“Can we pet him?” asked Charles, even though he guessed the answer.

“Not while he’s working,” said Ms. Danvers. “He will be in your classroom every day, keeping an eye on Luke. His job is very important to him, and he does not like to be distracted. But we’ll take a moment for him to get to know each of you after we've talked for a little while."

Sure enough, Hugo stuck to Luke's side like glue as they all returned to the solar system rug and sat down to hear more about Luke's new dog.

"Hugo is trained to take action if Luke has a seizure," explained Ms. Danvers. "He'll bark to let others know what's going on. He might place himself so that Luke won't get hurt if he falls down. If Luke has a seizure at night, Hugo will let his parents know. And he'll be there when the seizure is over, to comfort Luke."

"It means a lot more freedom for Luke," said Luke's mom. "If I know Hugo is with him, I don't have to worry."

"Yesss!" said Luke, pumping a fist. "Freedom!" He grinned down at his new friend, and Hugo gazed back at him, thumping his tail.

Bethany raised her hand. "Can Hugo tell when Luke is going to have a seizure? I mean, before it happens?"

"That's a great question," said Ms. Danvers. "Some seizure dogs do develop that ability. It's not something we can train a dog to do, but once a dog and owner have been together for a while, some extra-sensitive dogs do learn to notice the tiny signs that might come before a seizure. Then they can be even more helpful, nudging a person toward a chair, for example."

Charles watched Hugo, who was watching Luke. The dog's deep brown eyes seemed to notice everything. He had a feeling that Hugo would be one of the dogs who developed that skill. He was like Daisy, who always seemed to know what Charles was thinking or feeling.

Daisy. Charles had almost forgotten to be sad that Luke's family would not be adopting her after all. Now, watching Hugo, he had another, even better idea.

After all the explaining, Ms. Danvers said that she wanted to introduce Hugo to each of the kids in class. Mr. Mason told everyone to sit at their desks and do some silent reading while Ms. Danvers called them up one by one. Instead of paying attention to his book, Charles watched his classmates pet Hugo and ask Luke and Ms. Danvers questions. He could already tell that "Pukey Diaper" was history. With Hugo around, Luke was going to be the most popular kid in room 2B.

When Charles's turn came, he stroked Hugo's beautiful head while Hugo snuffled at his hand. "Ms. Danvers," he whispered. He knew he only had a moment to talk to her, so he got right to the point. "My family is fostering a puppy who might be perfect as a seizure dog."

She raised her eyebrows. "We're always interested in good candidates for our training," she said. She reached into her pocket and pulled out a business card. "Send me an email and tell me more about this puppy."

Charles held the card carefully. "I will," he said. "As soon as I get home from school."

She smiled. "I'll be waiting to hear from you."

Charles gave Hugo one more pat, then headed back to his seat, beaming. Even if Luke couldn't adopt her, Daisy might be able to help another kid with epilepsy. How great would that be?

CHAPTER NINE

Charles burst into his mom's study that afternoon as soon as he got home from school, waving the business card. "This is so perfect," he said.

"Hello to you, too," said his mom. "What is that?" She held out her hand for the card. "Laura Danvers, Happy Helpers. Where did you meet this person?"

Charles explained everything — about meeting Hugo, and about seizure dogs, and how he just knew that Daisy would be perfect for the job, and how he'd talked to Ms. Danvers. "So she said we should write her, and I told her I would, right away." He knelt to pet Daisy, who lay peacefully under his mom's desk. "I'm going to write and tell her all about you," he said to the puppy. Then he jumped up again. "Can you type while I talk?" he asked his mom. "Please? Pretty please?" He hopped around her chair.

Mom laughed. "I'll help type the e-mail, but I want you to write the letter first, by hand. I want you to take some time to think about what to tell this woman. Why would Daisy be a good seizure dog?"

"Because she's so smart," burst out Charles. "And she likes to be with people all the time, and she always seems to know how I'm feeling, and —"

Mom held up a hand. "Write it down," she said. "I don't care about your spelling or punctuation, but write it down. Then I'll help type it up and send it off. Deal?" She stuck out her hand.

Charles shook. "Deal." He grabbed a pencil and

put some paper on a clipboard. "Come on, Daisy," he said. "I'll take you out back, then we'll write a letter all about how wonderful you are." He scooped the little pup into his arms.

"She is pretty wonderful," Mom said. "She's been a good girl today. She behaves just fine as long as I don't leave her alone. My only complaint is that she snores so loudly when she's napping under my desk." She tickled Daisy under her chin. "Don't you, little girl?"

Daisy blinked as she snuffled at Mom's hand.

Nobody's perfect!

Charles took Daisy and Buddy out back for a while, then went inside and settled onto the couch to write his letter. Both dogs lay at his feet, Daisy chewing on a Kong toy that she had not yet been able to destroy.

Charles tapped the pencil against his teeth as he thought about how to begin. After a little while, he wrote:

Dear Ms. Danvers, I am Charles Peterson, a boy in Luke Piper's class. When I met you today, I told you about my foster puppy. Her name is Daisy and she is a Boston terrier. I think she is about six months old. She is very smart and sweet.

He looked down at Daisy. "You are, you know," he said. "If I were Wilma's daughter, I never would have given you up, no matter how much trouble you caused."

Daisy's stubby tail wiggled as she gazed back at him, her bulgy eyes shining. She panted a bit and gave Charles a funny doggy grin.

I'm glad you understand how special I am.

Charles had to get off the couch and hug Daisy for a little while before he could keep writing. Then Buddy got jealous, so he had to hug Buddy, too. “Okay, you guys,” he said, standing up again. “I have serious business to do here.” He sat down, picked up the clipboard again, and went back to writing.

Daisy is very sensitive. She seems to know how I am feeling and what I am thinking. She likes to be with me — or somebody — all the time. She knows how to sit and stay and come, and she hardly ever barks, unless she has a really good reason.

Charles shook out his hand. Was there anything else he needed to say? He thought of all the things Daisy had destroyed. It wasn't important to tell about that, was it? She was doing so well, anyway. Maybe she had already grown out of her destructive phase.

I hope you will consider taking Daisy into your training program. I think she could be a wonderful companion for somebody with epilepsy.

Sincerely, Charles Peterson

He signed his name extra big, just for fun, and drew three lines underneath it. "Done," he said.

Down at his feet, both dogs were fast asleep. Buddy lay curled up close to his new friend. Daisy snored gently and her ears twitched. They were so cute that Charles hated to wake them. He tip-toed out of the room and up the stairs to his mom's office.

"I'm all finished," he said, holding up the clipboard.

Mom read the letter. "Very good," she said. "You really have a way with words."

Charles blushed. It meant a lot when Mom said that, since she was a professional writer.

But Mom wasn't done. "There's only one problem. Daisy isn't quite as perfect as you make her sound. Don't you think we should tell Ms. Danvers about her destructive side? It's almost like lying if we don't."

"I guess," Charles said. "But she's gotten so much better."

"We'll say that, too," Mom promised.

Charles sat down next to her as she typed his letter into an e-mail, adding a sentence or two about Daisy's behavior problem. She read it back to him when she was done. "Ready to send it?" she asked.

Charles nodded, and Mom hit the "send" button. He leaned back in his seat and stretched. Now all he had to do was wait to hear back.

"Where's Daisy?" Mom asked.

"She's sleeping downstairs." Charles got up. "I'll go check on her." He trotted downstairs and into the living room. There was Buddy, still lying on the floor. And there was Daisy, sitting in the center of the biggest Daisy bomb yet: in the middle of the floor was one of the couch cushions with its fluffy white stuffing bulging out. Bits of fluff were strewn all over the rug. Charles put his hands to his mouth. "Daisy!" he said.

She looked up at him, all innocent. A piece of pillow stuffing hung out of her mouth.

Yes?

"Arrgh!" said Charles. He shooed Daisy off the cushion, then picked it up, turning it over to see how bad the damage really was. The bottom side was still mostly in one piece. He turned the cushion so that side was up and put it back onto the couch. He was gathering all the other fluffy pieces when Mom came clattering down the stairs. Quickly, he stuck them in his pocket.

Mom didn't seem to notice that anything was wrong. "Charles," she said. "Ms. Danvers already wrote back. She wants to come meet Daisy!"

CHAPTER TEN

"She wants to come over?" Charles tried not to look at the pillow. That would just draw Mom's attention to it. He knew he should tell her, but he just couldn't. Not right then. He picked Daisy up and moved away from the couch. "When? Like right this minute?"

Mom followed him and sat down on Dad's easy chair. "I'm supposed to call her. She can be here in half an hour, if I say it's okay. She said she's only in town for today. She covers all of New England, so she's very busy and always on the road. She said she was hoping to hear from you before she left."

Charles kissed the top of Daisy's head. "Wow," he said. He had hoped for a little more time. Of course he wanted to find the right home for Daisy — but couldn't they keep her a little longer? She was such a funny little thing. Plus, she still needed more training. Daisy was not the perfect dog. Not yet. Nobody knew that better than he did. The couch . . . He swallowed, holding that secret inside. "That's kind of . . . soon."

"I know," said Mom. "She sounded excited."

Charles tried to sound excited, too. "Great!"

"Maybe this will actually work out." Mom reached to scratch between Daisy's ears, and Daisy wrinkled up her face in a goofy smile. "Daisy really is a terrific little dog. And she hasn't destroyed anything in a few days."

Charles swallowed. "I know, she's really the best," he said. His stomach twisted. Daisy hadn't exactly *destroyed* the couch cushion. Not completely, anyway. It still looked okay on one side, didn't it? He snuck a glance at the couch. It looked fine. He would tell Mom about it right after the meeting with Ms. Danvers. They would probably laugh about it together. "Okay, let's call her." It would be better to get the meeting over with before Dad, Lizzie, and the Bean came home and complicated things. What if one of them went to sit on the couch?

Charles took Daisy and Buddy out back while Mom made the call. It couldn't hurt to have Daisy run a little bit and work off some energy. He wanted Ms. Danvers to see Daisy at her best. The puppies charged around the yard, first with Buddy chasing Daisy, then with Daisy chasing Buddy. Then Charles threw a ball for them until both dogs flopped down in the middle of the yard, panting. Charles lay between them, with a hand on each puppy, and closed his eyes for a few moments. Daisy scootched up under his arm and laid her head on his chest. She licked his chin gently, as if she could tell how nervous he was.

Everything will be fine. You'll see.

"Charles," called Mom. "Look who's here." She came out on the back deck, followed by Ms. Danvers.

Charles scrambled to his feet and wiped his hands on his pants. "Hi," he said.

"Hello," said Ms. Danvers. "Nice to see you again. And look at these two beautiful pups." She came right into the yard and knelt down to call the dogs. Both of them galloped over for pats and kisses. "I know you are Daisy," she said, chucking the bottom of Daisy's chin, "because you're a Boston terrier. But who are you?" She scratched between Buddy's ears.

"That's Buddy," said Charles. "He's ours. I mean, we're not just fostering him. He's in our family." He did not want Ms. Danvers to get the wrong idea. Buddy was a terrific dog — but he was *their* dog.

Ms. Danvers smiled. "I understand," she said. Then she got right down to business. "Let's talk about Daisy. I liked what you said about her in your e-mail."

"She's really great," Charles said. "There's only one thing I've been wondering. Is she too small to be a seizure dog?" That thought had been bothering him. Hugo was a big, beautiful dog, and Charles knew that Labs and German shepherds were the usual breeds for helping people.

"No way," said Ms. Danvers. "Small is beautiful. And for some people — like someone who lives in a tiny apartment, for example — a small dog is perfect." She stroked Daisy's short coat. "We placed a Boston terrier with a young woman last year. They're doing really well together. I have a picture of them in the scrapbook I brought to show you."

They went inside to look at the scrapbook. When Mom started for the living room, Charles's stomach twisted into a knot and his whole body felt hot. He never should have hidden the truth about the couch. What could he do? It was too late now. Everything was going so well. He did not want to ruin Daisy's chances. "Let's sit in the kitchen," he blurted out. "It — it'll be easier."

Mom gave him a funny look. "Okay," she said. She offered Ms. Danvers some cider and put out a plate of cookies.

Charles paged through the scrapbook, feeling almost like crying when he looked at the pictures. You could just tell how much love there was between the owners and their dogs. Daisy deserved that kind of love, and she had plenty to give in return. Charles hoped that Ms. Danvers would see that.

Daisy was on her best behavior. She didn't climb into Ms. Danvers's lap until she was invited. Then she snorted and snuffled and licked the woman's chin. Even though Ms. Danvers was all business, Charles could tell that she really loved dogs. He thought everything was going really well — until Ms. Danvers asked the question he did not want to hear. "So, little Miss Daisy. I hear you like to tear things up?"

Daisy blinked her bulgy eyes and grinned up at Ms. Danvers. She looked as innocent as ever.

Charles sighed. "Well, she doesn't like to be alone so much," he admitted.

"To be exact," his mom added, "when she is alone, she can be . . . well, destructive. But we've been working with her, and she's already much, much better."

Charles had felt his secret building up inside him ever since he had discovered the chewed-up couch cushion. Now it burst out. "She's better," he said. "But she still needs a lot of work." He got up from the table. "There's something I have to show you," he said, leading them into the living room. He knew this would probably wreck everything, but he couldn't hide the truth any longer.

He flipped over the couch cushion.

Mom gasped.

"I'm really sorry," said Charles. "It was my fault for leaving Daisy alone. I'll pay to fix it out of my allowance. And I'm sorry I didn't tell you. I just — I just really wanted Daisy to have this chance." He turned to Ms. Danvers, expecting her to look as shocked as Mom did.

Ms. Danvers just laughed. "That's pretty bad," she said. "But I've seen much, much worse. Believe me, Daisy won't have a moment to get into trouble like this once she starts our program. She'll be with a trainer all the time, and they'll be working hard."

Charles stared at her. "You mean . . ."

"And then," Charles told Luke on the phone later that night, "she said she had a really good feeling about Daisy, and she could tell that everything I had said in my letter was true, and Daisy would probably make a great seizure dog."

"That's awesome," said Luke. "I can't believe how fast it all happened."

"I know," said Charles. "The best part is that we get to keep her a little longer. The next training cycle doesn't start for a week, and Ms. Danvers will come pick her up then." He pulled Daisy onto his lap for a hug. She snuffled against his cheek and sighed with contentment.

When you're happy, I'm happy.

Charles sighed, too. Everything had worked out perfectly. Someday Daisy was going to help some other person with epilepsy the way Hugo was helping Luke. That was worth a hundred couch cushions, wasn't it?

PUPPY TIPS

In real life it's probably not quite so easy or quick for a dog to get accepted into a training program the way Daisy did. Some organizations breed their own dogs for training or take only certain kinds of dogs. Some use foster families to raise puppies for a year or so before they are old enough to be trained for a specific task, such as being a Seeing Eye dog. Other organizations do accept mixed-breed dogs and dogs of all sizes. Your parents can help you learn more about helping dogs by looking online. Be sure to watch some of the videos about helping dogs and their owners. They are amazing!

Dear Reader,

Not every dog can become an official helping dog, but most pups are sensitive to their owners' moods. If I am upset or crying, my dog Zipper will come over to lean against me and lick my face. Sometimes he'll bring me one of his toys or show me one of his tricks. It always cheers me up to have him nearby. Just another reason I love dogs!

Yours from the Puppy Place,

Ellen Miles

ABOUT THE AUTHOR

Ellen Miles loves dogs, which is why she has a great time writing the Puppy Place books. And guess what? She loves cats, too! (In fact, her very first pet was a beautiful tortoiseshell cat named Jenny.) That's why she came up with the Kitty Corner series. Ellen lives in Vermont and loves to be outdoors every day, walking, biking, skiing, or swimming, depending on the season. She also loves to read, cook, explore her beautiful state, play with dogs, and hang out with friends and family.

Visit Ellen at www.ellenmiles.net.

THE PUPPY PLACE

DON'T MISS THE NEXT PUPPY PLACE ADVENTURE!

Here's a peek at GUS!

"What are you talking about?" Lizzie glared at Daphne. "Why would we need a different president?"

Daphne shrugged. "Maybe it's just time for a change."

Lizzie did not agree. Why did they need to change anything? Everything was working just fine. She looked around the table at Maria and

Brianna. Maria, her best friend, did not look back at her. Brianna was looking at Daphne — *her* best friend. Lizzie threw up her hands. "This wasn't even on our agenda for today," she said.

It was Friday afternoon, time for the weekly meeting of the AAA Dynamic Dog Walkers. As always, they were at the home of Lizzie Peterson, president. She was president for a lot of good reasons. Number one: she had invented the whole idea of the business and had lined up the very first clients. Number two: she knew the most about dogs. She had a library full of books about dogs and an aunt who ran a doggy day care. She volunteered every week at the local animal shelter, Caring Paws. On top of all that, her family fostered puppies. They took care of puppies who needed help until they found them fantastic forever homes. Number three: she had a lot of good ideas. Number four — Well, Lizzie couldn't think of number four just then, but only because Daphne had started talking again.

"It's, like, I just think maybe we need a breath of fresh air, some new ideas." Daphne looked at Brianna while she spoke, and Brianna nodded eagerly.

"Fresh air is great," said Lizzie, crossing her arms. "So are new ideas. But do we really need a different president to have those?" She looked at Maria, waiting for her to nod the way Brianna had nodded at Daphne.

Maria was still looking down at the kitchen table.